This book belongs to...

....

....

The Nursery Collection

Sing a Song of Sixpence

This is a Parragon Book
This edition published in 2003

Parragon, Queen Street House, 4 Queen Street, Bath BA1 1HE, UK

Produced by The Templar Company plc

Copyright © Parragon 2000

Edited by Caroline Repchuk
Designed by Kilnwood Graphics

Printed and bound in China
ISBN 1 40540 062 5

The Nursery Collection

Sing a Song of Sixpence

p

Contents

Oranges and Lemons

Oranges and lemons,

Say the bells of St Clements.

I owe you five farthings,

Say the bells of St Martins.

When will you pay me?

Say the bells of Old Bailey.

When I grow rich,

Say the bells of Shoreditch.

Rub-A-Dub-Dub

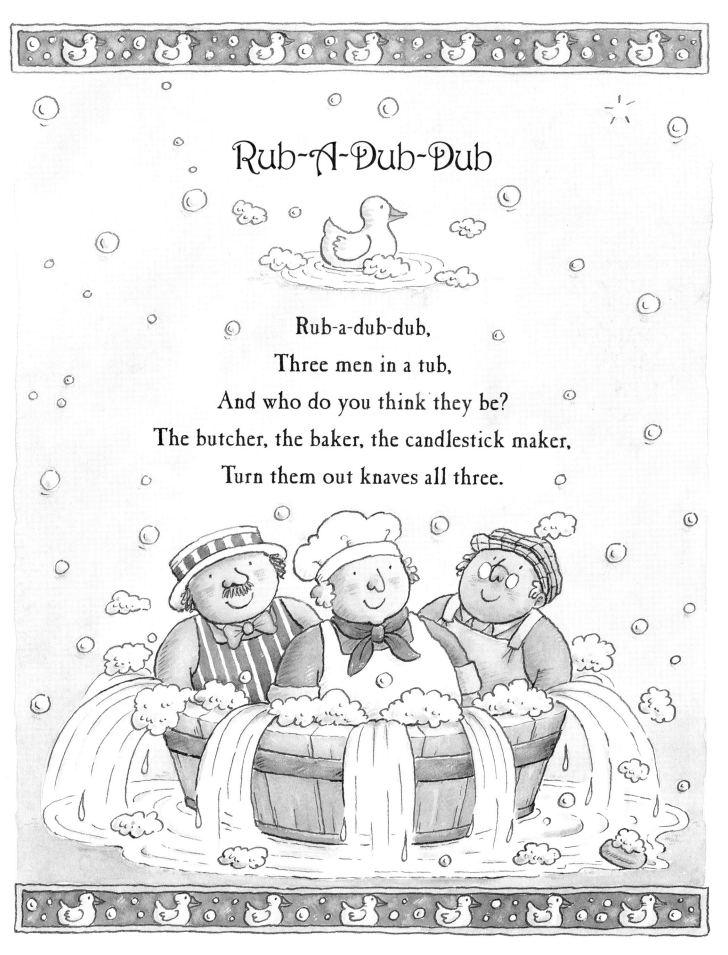

Rub-a-dub-dub,
Three men in a tub,
And who do you think they be?
The butcher, the baker, the candlestick maker,
Turn them out knaves all three.

Knick Knack Paddy Whack

This old man, he played one,

He played knick knack on my drum.

With a knick knack paddy whack, give a dog a bone,

This old man went rolling home.

This old man, he played two,

He played knick knack on my shoe.

With a knick knack paddy whack, give a dog a bone,

This old man went rolling home.

This old man, he played three,
He played knick knack on my knee.
With a knick knack paddy whack, give a dog a bone,
This old man went rolling home.

This old man, he played four,
He played knick knack on my door.
With a knick knack paddy whack, give a dog a bone,
This old man went rolling home.

This old man, he played five,
He played knick knack on my hive.
With a knick knack paddy whack, give a dog a bone,
This old man went rolling home.

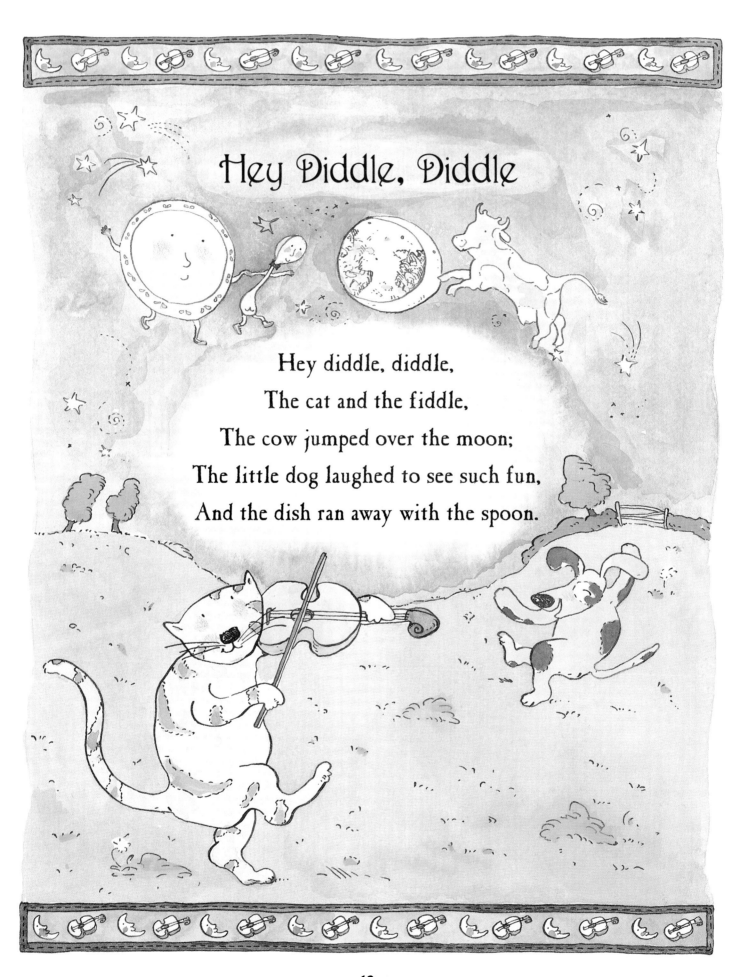

Hey Diddle, Diddle

Hey diddle, diddle,
The cat and the fiddle,
The cow jumped over the moon;
The little dog laughed to see such fun,
And the dish ran away with the spoon.

Little Bo Peep

Little Bo Peep has lost her sheep
And doesn't know where to find them;
Leave them alone, and they'll come home
Bringing their tails behind them.

Dance To Your Daddy

Dance to your daddy,
My little babby;
Dance to your daddy,
My little lamb.
You shall have a fishy
On a little dishy,
You shall have a fishy
When the boat comes in.

Humpty Dumpty

Humpty Dumpty sat on a wall;
Humpty Dumpty had a great fall;
All the King's horses, and all the King's men
Couldn't put Humpty together again.

The Owl and the Pussy-cat

The Owl and the Pussy-cat went to sea
In a beautiful pea-green boat,
They took some honey, and plenty of money,
Wrapped up in a five-pound note.
The Owl looked up to the stars above,
And sang to a small guitar,
"O lovely Pussy! O Pussy, my love,
What a beautiful Pussy you are,
You are, you are!
What a beautiful Pussy you are!"

Pussy said to the Owl, "You elegant fowl!

How charmingly sweet you sing!

"O let us be married! Too long we have tarried:

But what shall we do for a ring?"

They sailed away, for a year and a day,

To the land where the Bong-tree grows,

And there in a wood a Piggy-wig stood,

With a ring at the end of his nose,

His nose, his nose,

With a ring at the end of his nose.

"Dear Pig, are you willing to sell for one shilling
Your ring?" Said the Piggy, "I will."
So they took it away, and were married next day
By the Turkey who lives on the hill.

They dined on mince, and slices of quince,
Which they ate with a runcible spoon;
And hand in hand, on the edge of the sand,
They danced by the light of the moon,
The moon, the moon,
They danced by the light of the moon.

Goosey Goosey Gander

Goosey, goosey, gander,

Whither shall I wander?

Upstairs and downstairs,

And in my lady's chamber.

There I met an old man

Who would not say his prayers.

I took him by the left leg

And threw him down the stairs.

Where are you Going to My Pretty Maid?

Where are you going to, my pretty maid?
Where are you going to, my pretty maid?
I'm going a-milking, sir, she said,
Sir, she said, sir, she said,
I'm going a-milking, sir, she said.

May I go with you, my pretty maid?
May I go with you, my pretty maid?
You're kindly welcome, sir, she said,
Sir, she said, sir, she said,
You're kindly welcome, sir, she said.

What is your fortune, my pretty maid?

What is your fortune, my pretty maid?

My face is my fortune, sir, she said,

Sir, she said, sir, she said,

My face is my fortune, sir, she said.

Then I can't marry you, my pretty maid,

Then I can't marry you, my pretty maid,

Nobody asked you, sir, she said,

Sir, she said, sir, she said,

Nobody asked you, sir, she said.

London Bridge is Falling Down

London bridge is falling down,
Falling down, falling down,
London bridge is falling down,
My fair lady.

Build it up with wood and clay,
Wood and clay, wood and clay,
Build it up with wood and clay,
My fair lady

Wood and clay will wash away,
Wash away, wash away,
Wood and clay will wash away,
My fair lady.

Build it up with bricks and mortar,
Bricks and mortar, bricks and mortar,
Build it up with bricks and mortar,
My fair lady.

Bricks and mortar will not stay,
Will not stay, will not stay,
Bricks and mortar will not stay,
My fair lady.

Build it up with iron and steel,
Iron and steel, iron and steel,
Build it up with iron and steel,
My fair lady.

Iron and steel will bend and bow,
Bend and bow, bend and bow
Iron and steel will bend and bow,
My fair lady.

Build it up with silver and gold,
Silver and gold, silver and gold,
Build it up with silver and gold,
My fair lady.

Silver and gold will be stolen away,
Stolen away, stolen away,
Silver and gold will be stolen away,
My fair lady.

Set a man to watch all night,
Watch all night, watch all night,
Set a man to watch all night,
My fair lady.

Girls and Boys

Girls and boys come out to play,

The moon doth shine as bright as day,

Leave your supper and leave your sleep,

And come with your playfellows into the street.

Come with a whoop, come with a call,

Come with a good will, or come not at all.

Up the ladder and down the wall,

A halfpenny bun will serve us all.

You find milk and I'll find flour,

And we'll have pudding in half an hour.

One, Two, Three, Four, Five

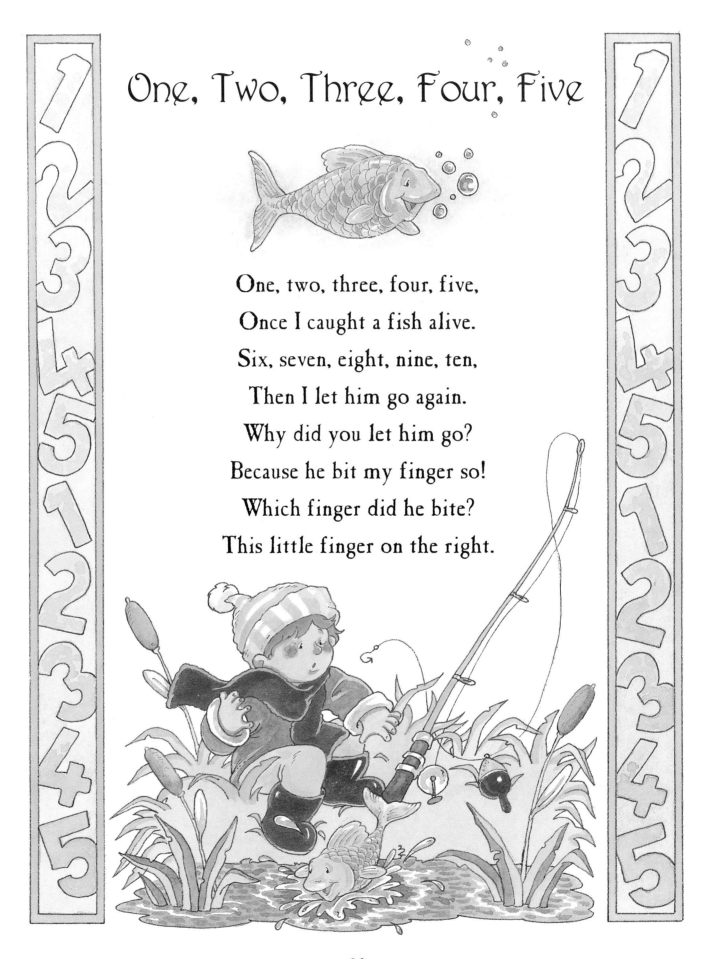

One, two, three, four, five,

Once I caught a fish alive.

Six, seven, eight, nine, ten,

Then I let him go again.

Why did you let him go?

Because he bit my finger so!

Which finger did he bite?

This little finger on the right.

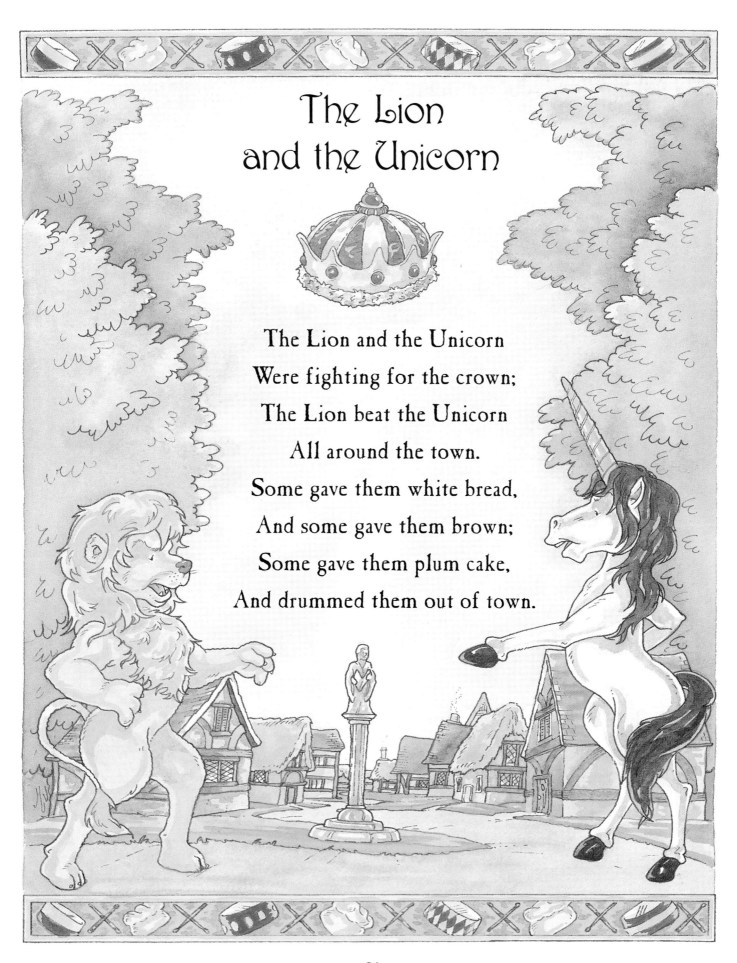

The Lion
and the Unicorn

The Lion and the Unicorn
Were fighting for the crown;
The Lion beat the Unicorn
All around the town.
Some gave them white bread,
And some gave them brown;
Some gave them plum cake,
And drummed them out of town.

Lucy Locket

Lucy Locket lost her pocket,
Kitty Fisher found it.
Not a penny was there in it,
Only ribbon round it.

Cinderella's umbrella's
Full of holes all over.
Every time it starts to rain
She has to run for cover.

Aladdin's lamp is getting damp,
And is no longer gleaming.
It doesn't spark within the dark,
But you can't stop it steaming.

I Love Little Pussy

I love little pussy,
her coat is so warm,
And if I don't hurt her
she'll do me no harm.
So I'll not pull her tail,
nor drive her away,
But Pussy and I very
gently will play.

I Had a Little Nut Tree

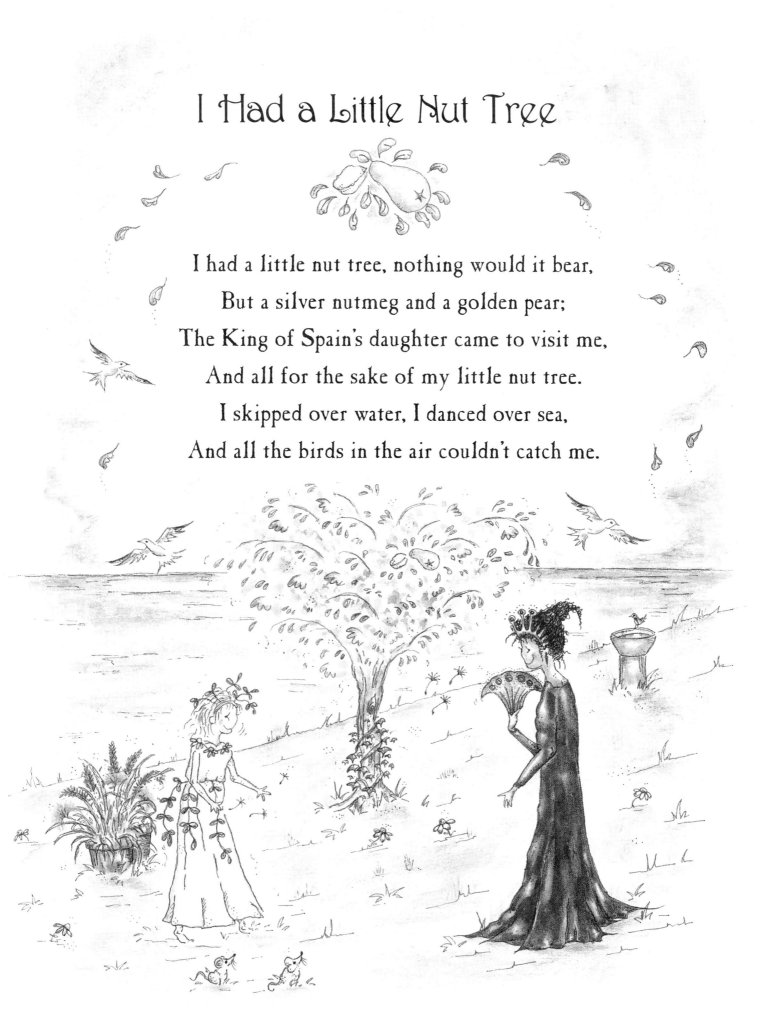

I had a little nut tree, nothing would it bear,

But a silver nutmeg and a golden pear;

The King of Spain's daughter came to visit me,

And all for the sake of my little nut tree.

I skipped over water, I danced over sea,

And all the birds in the air couldn't catch me.

Simple Simon

Simple Simon met a pieman
Going to the fair,
Says Simple Simon to the pieman
"Let me taste your ware."
Says the pieman to Simple Simon,
"Show me first your penny."
Says Simple Simon to the pieman,
"Indeed I have not any."

Simple Simon went a-fishing
For to catch a whale;
But all the water he had got
Was in his mother's pail.

One Man Went To Mow

One man went to mow, went to mow a meadow,
One man and his dog, Spot,
Went to mow a meadow.

Two men went to mow, went to mow a meadow,
Two men, one man and his dog, Spot,
Went to mow a meadow.

Three men went to mow, went to mow a meadow,
Three men, two men, one man and his dog, Spot,
Went to mow a meadow.

Four men went to mow, went to mow a meadow,
Four men, three men, two men, one man and his dog, Spot,
Went to mow a meadow.

Five men went to mow, went to mow a meadow,
Five men, four men, three men, two men,
one man and his dog, Spot,
Went to mow a meadow.

There Was a Crooked Man

There was a crooked man
And he walked a crooked mile,
He found a crooked sixpence
Against a crooked stile.
He brought a crooked cat
Which caught a crooked mouse
And they all lived together
In a little crooked house.

Baa Baa Black Sheep

Baa, baa, black sheep,
Have you any wool?
Yes, sir, yes, sir,
Three bags full;
One for the master,
And one for the dame,
And one for the little boy
Who lives down the lane.

Hot Cross Buns!

Hot cross buns!

Hot cross buns!

One a-penny, two a-penny,

Hot cross buns!

If you have no daughters,

Give them to your sons,

One a-penny, two a-penny,

Hot cross buns!

Old MacDonald

Old Macdonald had a farm,

E...I...E...I...O

And on that farm he had some cows,

E...I...E...I...O

With a moo-moo here,

And a moo-moo there,

Here a moo, there a moo,

Everywhere a moo-moo,

Old Macdonald had a farm,

E...I...E...I...O

Old Macdonald had a farm,

E...I...E...I...O

And on that farm he had some ducks,

E...I...E...I...O

With a quack-quack here,

And a quack-quack there, *etc.*

This rhyme can be continued with other verses: sheep, baa-baa; dogs, woof-woof; horses, neigh-neigh; cats, miaow-miaow; etc. The speed can be adjusted to suit the age of the child. Older children can memorise the previous verses and add them to the rhyme, eg. 'with a quack-quack here, and a quack-quack there, here a quack, there a quack, everywhere a quack, quack, moo-moo here, moo-moo there,' etc.

Oh Dear, What Can The Matter Be?

Oh dear, what can the matter be?

Dear, dear, what can the matter be?

Oh dear, what can the matter be?

Johnny's so long at the fair.

He promised he'd buy me a basket of posies,

A garland of lilies, a garland of roses,

A little straw hat to set off the blue ribbons

That tie up my bonny brown hair.

Oh dear, what can the matter be?

Dear, dear, what can the matter be?

Oh dear, what can the matter be?

Johnny's so long at the fair.

Jack and Jill

Jack and Jill went up the hill
To fetch a pail of water;
Jack fell down and broke his crown
And Jill came tumbling after.

Up Jack got and home did trot
As fast as he could caper;
He went to bed to mend his head
With vinegar and brown paper.

Polly Put The Kettle On

Polly put the kettle on,

Polly put the kettle on,

Polly put the kettle on,

We'll all have tea.

Sukey take it off again,

Sukey take it off again,

Sukey take it off again,

They've all gone away.

Cock-a-Doodle-Doo

Cock-a-doodle-doo!

My dame has lost her shoe,

My master's lost his fiddling stick,

And doesn't know what to do.

Cock-a-doodle-doo!

What is my dame to do?

Till master finds his fiddling stick,

She'll dance without her shoe.

Cock-a-doodle-doo!

My dame has found her shoe,

And master's found his fiddling stick,

Sing cock-a-doodle-doo.

Pussy Cat, Pussy Cat

Pussy cat, pussy cat, where have you been?

I've been up to London to visit the Queen.

Pussy cat, pussy cat, what did you there?

I frightened a little mouse under her chair.

Diddle, Diddle, Dumpling

Diddle, diddle, dumpling, my son John,

Went to bed with his trousers on;

One shoe off, one shoe on,

Diddle, diddle, dumpling, my son John.

Hey de Ho

Hey de, hey de ho,
The great big elephant
Is so slow.
Hey de, hey de ho,
The elephant is so slow.

He swings his tail
From side to side,
As he takes the children
For a ride.

Hey de, hey de ho,
The elephant is so slow.

Georgie Porgie

Georgie Porgie, pudding and pie,
Kissed the girls and made them cry;
When the boys came out to play,
Georgie Porgie ran away.

Three Blind Mice

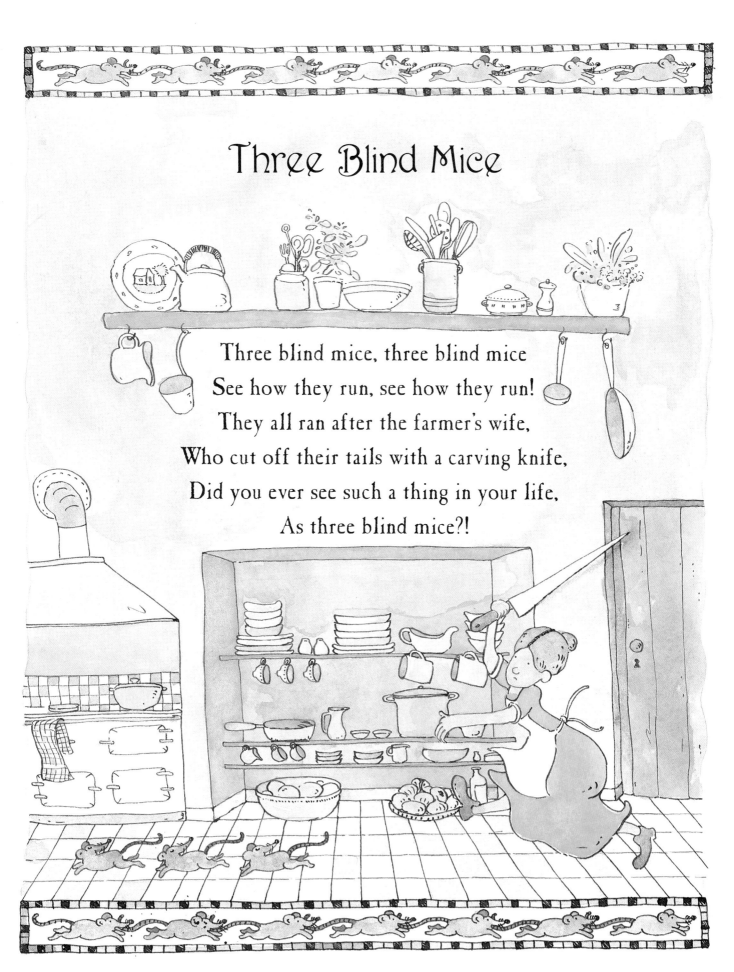

Three blind mice, three blind mice
See how they run, see how they run!
They all ran after the farmer's wife,
Who cut off their tails with a carving knife,
Did you ever see such a thing in your life,
As three blind mice?!

Ding Dong Bell

Ding, dong, bell,

Pussy's in the well!

Who put her in?

Little Tommy Green.

Who pulled her out?

Little Johnny Stout.

What a naughty boy was that

To try to drown poor pussy cat,

Who never did any harm,

But killed the mice in his father's barn.

A Frog He Would A-Wooing Go

A frog he would a-wooing go,

Heigho! says Rowley,

Whether his mother would let him or no,

With a rowley, powley, gammon and spinach,

Heigho! says Anthony Rowley.

So off he set with his opera hat,

Heigho! says Rowley,

And on the way he met with a rat,

With a rowley, powley, gammon and spinach,

Heigho! says Anthony Rowley.

Pray, Mister Rat, will you go with me?
Heigh ho! says Rowley,
Kind Mistress Mousey for to see?
With a rowley, powley, gammon and spinach,
Heigh ho! says Anthony Rowley.

They came to the door of Mousey's hall,
Heigh ho! says Rowley,
They gave a loud knock and they gave a loud call.
With a rowley, powley, gammon and spinach,
Heigh ho! says Anthony Rowley.

Pray, Mistress Mouse, will you give us some beer?
Heigh ho! says Rowley,
For Froggy and I are fond of good cheer.
With a rowley, powley, gammon and spinach,
Heigh ho! says Anthony Rowley.

But while they were all a merry-making,
Heigh ho! says Rowley,
A cat and her kittens came tumbling in.
With a rowley, powley, gammon and spinach,
Heigh ho! says Anthony Rowley.

The cat she seized the rat by the crown,
Heigh ho! says Rowley,
The kittens they pulled the little mouse down.
With a rowley, powley, gammon and spinach,
Heigh ho! says Anthony Rowley.

This put Mister Frog in a terrible fright.
Heigh ho! says Rowley,
He took up his hat and he wished them goodnight.
With a rowley, powley, gammon and spinach,
Heigh ho! says Anthony Rowley.

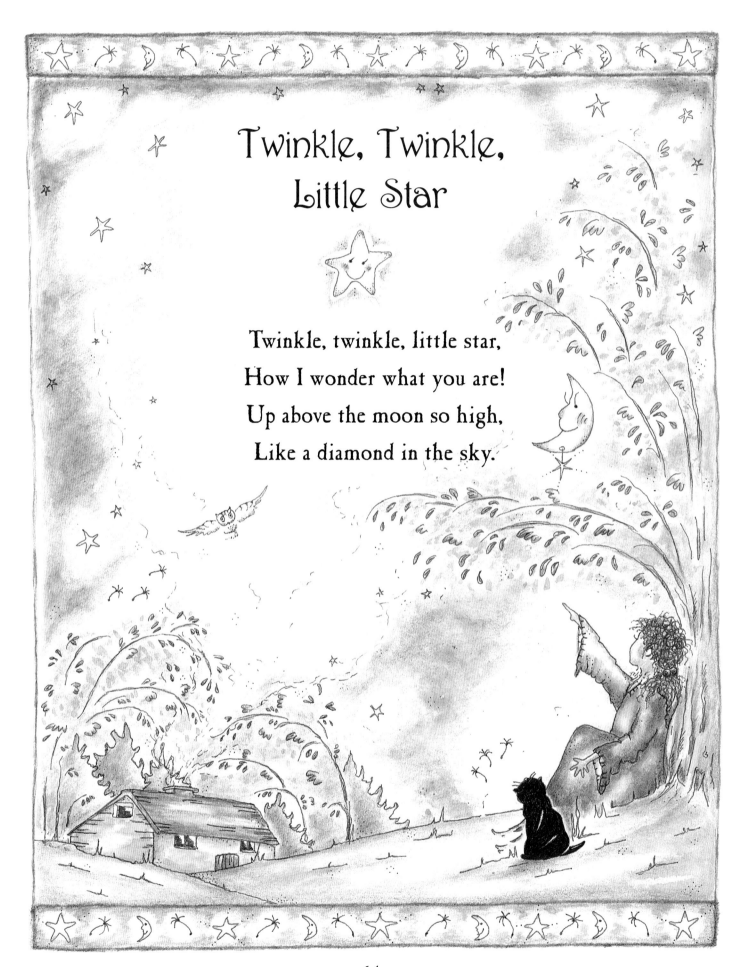

Twinkle, Twinkle, Little Star

Twinkle, twinkle, little star,
How I wonder what you are!
Up above the moon so high,
Like a diamond in the sky.

Ride A Cock-Horse

Ride a cock-horse to Banbury Cross,

To see a fine lady upon a white horse,

With rings on her fingers and bells on her toes

She shall have music wherever she goes.

Grand Old Duke of York

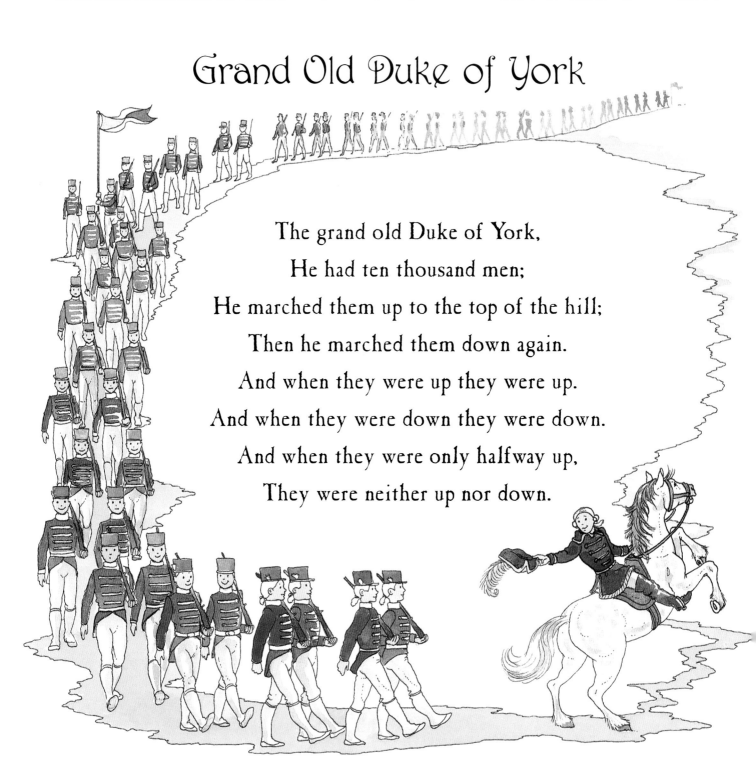

The grand old Duke of York,

He had ten thousand men;

He marched them up to the top of the hill;

Then he marched them down again.

And when they were up they were up.

And when they were down they were down.

And when they were only halfway up,

They were neither up nor down.

Bye, Baby Bunting

Bye, Baby Bunting

Daddy's gone a-hunting,

To find a little rabbit skin,

To wrap his Baby Bunting in.

Old Mother Hubbard

Old Mother Hubbard
Went to the cupboard
To fetch her poor dog a bone,
But when she got there
The cupboard was bare
And so the poor dog had none.

Tom, Tom The Piper's Son

Tom, Tom, the piper's son,
Stole a pig and away he run!
The pig was eat, and Tom was beat,
And Tom went roaring down the street.

Little Boy Blue

Little Boy Blue, come blow your horn

The sheep's in the meadow, the cow's in the corn.

Where is the boy who looks after the sheep?

He's under the haystack fast asleep.

Will you wake him? No, not I!

For if I do, he's sure to cry.

Yankee Doodle

Yankee Doodle came to town,
Riding on a pony,
He stuck a feather in his cap
And called it macaroni.

Bobby Shaftoe

Bobby Shaftoe's gone to sea,
Silver buckles at his knee,
He'll come back and marry me,
Bonny Bobby Shaftoe.

Little Jack Horner

Little Jack Horner,
Sat in a corner,
Eating a Christmas pie.
He put in his thumb,
And pulled out a plum,
And said, "What a good boy am I!"

Ten Green Bottles

Ten green bottles, standing on a wall,

Ten green bottles, standing on a wall,

And if one green bottle should accidentally fall,

There'd be nine green bottles, standing on a wall.

(continue with nine green bottles etc...)

Frère Jacques

Frère Jacques, Frère Jacques
Dormez-vous, dormez-vous?
Sonnez les matines, sonnez les matines,
Ding, dang, dong, ding, dang, dong.

Little Miss Muffet

Little Miss Muffet
Sat on a tuffet,
Eating her curds and whey;
There came a big spider,
Who sat down beside her,
And frightened Miss Muffet away.

Wee Willie Winkie

Wee Willie Winkie runs through the town,

Upstairs and downstairs in his nightgown,

Rapping at the windows, crying through the locks,

"Are the children in their beds,

It's past eight o'clock?"

Mary, Mary, Quite Contrary

Mary, Mary, quite contrary,
How does your garden grow?
With silver bells and cockle shells
And pretty maids all in a row.

A Tisket, A Tasket

A tisket, a tasket,
A green and yellow basket.
I wrote a letter to my love,
And on the way I dropped it.

I dropped it, I dropped it,
And on the way I dropped it.
A little girl picked it up
And put it in her pocket.

Pease Pudding Hot

Pease pudding hot,
Pease pudding cold,
Pease pudding in the pot,
Nine days old.

Some like it hot,
Some like it cold,
Some like it in the pot,
Nine days old.

Sing a Song of Sixpence

Sing a song of sixpence,
A pocket full of rye;
Four-and-twenty blackbirds baked in a pie;
When the pie was opened,
The birds began to sing;
Wasn't that a dainty dish,
To set before a king?

Lazy Mary

Lazy Mary will you get up,

Will you get up, will you get up?

Lazy Mary will you get up,

Will you get up today?

Six o'clock and you're still sleeping,

Daylight's creeping o'er your windowsill.

Lazy Mary will you get up,

Will you get up, will you get up?

Lazy Mary will you get up,

Will you get up today?

Seven o'clock and you're still snoring,
Sunshine's pouring through your window pane.

Lazy Mary will you get up,
Will you get up, will you get up?
Lazy Mary will you get up,
Will you get up today?

Eight o'clock, you've missed your train,
Can you explain why you're still in your bed?

Higgledy-Piggledy

Higgledy-Piggledy,
My black hen,
She lays eggs for gentlemen;
Sometimes nine,
And sometimes ten,
Higgledy-Piggledy, my black hen!

Oats and Beans

Oats and beans and barley grow,
Oats and beans and barley grow,
Do you or I or anyone know,
How oats and beans and barley grow?

First the farmer sows his seeds,
Then he stands and takes his ease,
Stamps his feet and claps his hands,
Turns around to view the land.

The Muffin Man

Have you seen the muffin man,
The muffin man, the muffin man?
Have you seen the muffin man,
He lives in Drury Lane?
Oh yes, I've seen the muffin man,
The muffin man, the muffin man.
Oh yes, I've seen the muffin man,
He lives in Drury Lane.

Old King Cole

Old King Cole was a merry old soul,
And a merry old soul was he;
He called for his pipe,
And he called for his bowl,
And he called for his fiddlers three.

The Man In The Moon

The man in the moon
Came down too soon,
And asked his way to Norwich;
He went by the south,
And burnt his mouth
By eating cold plum porridge.

Rock-a-Bye-Baby

Rock-a-bye baby, on the tree top;

When the wind blows, the cradle will rock;

When the bough breaks, the cradle will fall;

Down will come baby, cradle and all.

It's Raining, It's Pouring

It's raining, it's pouring,
The old man is snoring.
He went to bed,
And bumped his head,
And couldn't get up
in the morning.

Lavender's Blue

Lavender's blue, dilly, dilly, lavender's green,

When I am king, dilly, dilly, you shall be queen;

Call up your men, dilly dilly, set them to work,

Some to the plough, dilly dilly, some to the cart;

Some to make hay, dilly, dilly, some to thresh corn;

Whilst you and I, dilly, dilly, keep ourselves warm.

The Farmer's in his Den

The farmer's in his den,
The farmer's in his den,
E I E I
The farmer's in his den.

The farmer wants a wife,
The farmer wants a wife,
E I E I
The farmer wants a wife.

The wife wants a child,
The wife wants a child,
E I E I
The wife wants a child.

The child wants a nurse,

The child wants a nurse,

E I E I

The child wants a nurse.

The nurse wants a dog,

The nurse wants a dog,

E I E I

The nurse wants a dog.

We all pat the dog,

We all pat the dog,

E I E I

We all pat the dog.

Dancing Round the Maypole

Dancing round the maypole,

Dancing all the day,

Dancing round the maypole,

On the first of May,

Dancing round the maypole,

What a merry bunch,

Dancing round the maypole,

Till it's time for lunch.

Dancing round the maypole,
Shouting out with glee,
Dancing round the maypole,
Till it's time for tea.
Dancing round the maypole,
Blue and white and red,
Dancing round the maypole,
Till it's time for bed.

The End